A Month of Sundays

A Month of Sundays

A. E. BALL

RESOURCE *Publications* · Eugene, Oregon

A MONTH OF SUNDAYS

Resource Publications
An Imprint of Wipf and Stock Publishers
199 W. 8th Ave., Suite 3
Eugene, OR 97401

www.wipfandstock.com

PAPERBACK ISBN: 979-8-3852-1043-5
HARDCOVER ISBN: 979-8-3852-1044-2
EBOOK ISBN: 979-8-3852-1045-9

All biblical quotations are from the 1995 version of the New American Standard Bible.

This book is a work of fiction. Names, characters, places, and events herein are either the product of the author's imagination or are used fictitiously. Any resemblance to actual persons, living or deceased, is wholly coincidental.

Dedicated to Kenny and Jessica,
in expectant hope that you will be there.

I want to acknowledge and thank the talented team that assisted me in bringing this project together: Nate Hitchcock, Katherine Burge, Shelby Kiper Burns, and Jude Cooper.

*If I go and prepare a place for you, I will come
again and receive you to Myself, that where I
am, there you may be also.*

—John 14:3

My Dear Friend,

It feels like a millennium has passed since we last spoke. It has
actually been much longer than that. Looking back on our times
together, it all seems so muddled. But then, I suppose that's because of the light and clarity with which I now live. To think that
we once considered ourselves to have grasped the truth is quite
astonishing indeed. We didn't know the half of it.

My purpose in writing is to tell you what to expect. I never
thought I'd have the opportunity to communicate from the future
to your "past self." The King has granted me permission to do this
because it cannot alter anything now. He already knows you, and
I've seen your name in the Book of Life which is now eternally
open for review in the Great City. Recently, I traveled to view the
Book to find out where you now reside.

In any case, I am preparing this letter to arrive in the past
as well as a copy to your current residence here, in hopes that we
might get together again. I can hardly wait to see you in all your
perfection.

Now let me get on with revealing this place to you. Let me
begin by telling you where I live. It's affectionately known as Willow Bay. Doesn't that tell you everything? Oh, but allow me to fill
in some blanks.

Willow Bay sits on the bright banks of a lake called Cheer. It's where my sweet cottage and land were prepared for me long ago. The King knew exactly how to delight me. But then, here on New Earth's New Scotland, everything is a delight. I'm not even sure that delight is the right word for it though. Being here is more like those moments you had as a child when a shiver moved from your toes to your head and then out the top of you. Remember that sensation? It was a combination of glee, anticipation, and a feeling of overwhelming love and security. Even that's a pale description of the everlasting goosebump ecstasy we have here. But I digress.

Lake Cheer is in the heart of the Cheer District. The district is about one hundred square miles in size. My home is on one side of the oval-shaped Lake Cheer. Far off to my left (facing the lake) is a village called Grace. To my right is the city of Cheer—the very hub of the district. Directly opposite my place, across the lake, is a medium-sized town called Linger. It's aptly named because it's where everyone wants to linger before making their way toward the Great City. There are thousands of residents in the district— more in the cities and fewer in the countryside. I'll be sure to tell you about each town (as well as Willow Bay) later. However, I thought I should include in this "mailing" my hand-drawn map so that you get a better sense of the place.

By now your eyes have probably been drawn to the signature on this letter. Yes, it's really me . . . but from the very distant future. I know you can't believe this is happening. I'm certain I would have felt the same way receiving a letter from New Earth. You're probably also wondering why and how this could happen.

Let's start with the why. As mentioned earlier, I initially approached our loving King to ask if I could send these letters to a nonbelieving friend on the old earth. Of course, my hope was that he would become a believer as a result of the letters. As I sat at the foot of His throne, the King reminded me of His Word which stands forever and will never pass away. He said that if my friend would not heed His Word, then he would certainly not be persuaded by the Messiah being raised from the dead. And let's face it, my letters would be much less astounding than that.

However, the King did concede to my writing these letters to you because you already knew Him and, more importantly, He knew you from before the foundations of time. In fact, He said I could write thirty-one letters, and He would have each delivered on Sundays. I tried to tell Him that there was no postal service on Sundays in your part of the old earth, but He gave me that endearing glance that (once again) reminded me that He does as He will and by His Word. Greatest king ever!

So, my friend, that brings us to the how of the matter. You can expect to find a letter in your mailbox for the next thirty-one Sundays. This will take *months* in the old time-bound world, and I can only imagine how many questions you must have. I'll do my best to answer what I think may be on your mind—to the extent I am permitted or able to express. I'm about to finish up this letter, and a Messenger is coming to take it away. Looking forward to getting together with you here to find out what you thought about these letters back then.

Your friend forever,

Anne

P.S. I know you're probably thinking you should stand next to your mailbox next Sunday for twenty-four hours hoping to get a glimpse of a Messenger, but don't bother. After all, the King didn't need to send someone ahead to place a shekel in the mouth of that fish.

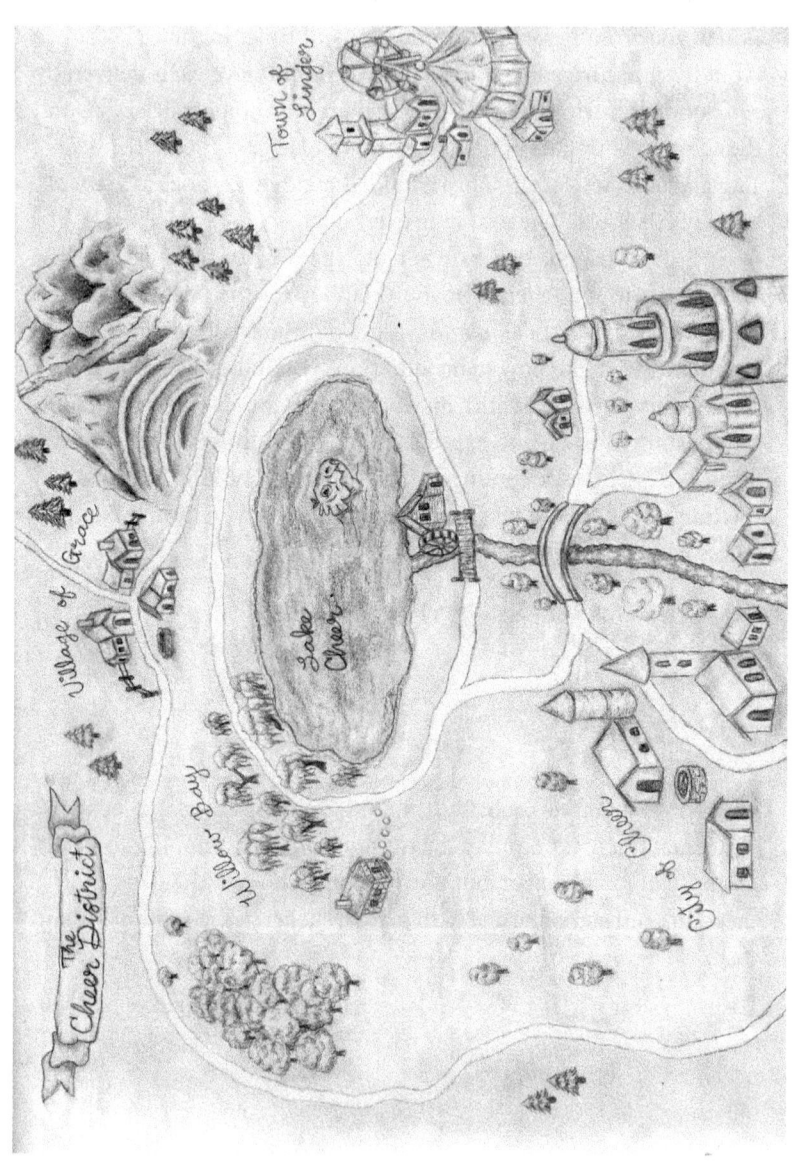

In My Father's house are many dwelling places; if it were not so,
I would have told you; for I go to prepare a place for you.
—John 14:2

My Dear Friend,

Hello again! It must be Sunday. I'm guessing you didn't find the first letter until this past Monday because who would be expecting mail on a Sunday?

In this letter, I've provided some details for you about the district where I reside on New Earth.

As previously mentioned, my cottage is in the Cheer District and situated on the banks of Lake Cheer. It's a stone construction with a thatched roof, includes a walk-in stone fireplace, and sits on a beautiful plot of land leading down to the lake. I can sit on my back porch, watching the forest of willow trees on one side of the property, and still have an open view of the lake. Those willow trees (and the double entendre) are why I named it Willow Bay. They sway in the light breeze and their drooping limbs each carry small blooms of various colors. Like so many things here on New Earth, the blossoms are an improvement over those from the old earth. There are shades of pastels, deep purple, orange, and even some colors that I can't describe because they can be perceived only with our glorified (enhanced) eyes.

I absolutely love my forever home. It's clear to all of us here that the King, who knows us completely, was preparing places we would each find delightful. The entire Cheer District is full of beautiful homes, each befitting its residents and all a joy to behold. I can't wait to visit you in your district to see how He has fashioned your place. I know a bit about your taste for what we used to call mid-century modern style, so I'm wondering if that's what you have in the Common District of New Italy.

As I reread the first paragraphs of this letter, I am mindful of how each sentence may trigger yet another question for you. I won't be able to anticipate and answer all questions, but let's take a quick detour on some of the above.

Is New Earth divided up into districts? Yes, and by country. All of them "new" because He made all things new. Hence, I live in New Scotland. Many live in the New Americas because they span from what used to be North, Central, and South America. Others make their home in New Australia, New Africa, or New Asia. Each location has traits, architecture, and vistas reminiscent of their old world, but each is vastly enhanced. There's a whole new world to explore, and I'll speak about travel in subsequent letters.

Does every location on New Earth have just one name? Yes, with the exception of your own property which you can name as you wish. All districts, towns, villages, cities, and hamlets were already named upon our arrival out of the Millennial Kingdom. New Jerusalem (which most refer to as the Great City) is home to the King. It's quite large, sprawling, and populated largely by those who were "blessed to be a blessing." That's not to say that there aren't what we formerly knew as "gentiles" living there too. There were many who chose to live there. However, those of us who have a home elsewhere are always visiting the Great City. More on that later.

You chose to live in New Italy? Yep—and who wouldn't? I hear it's gorgeous, and I'm going to visit you there soon. It will be my first time in New Italy. In fact, I may have more to report on that in my next letter since we'll likely be meeting up before I sit down to write it.

Back to the Cheer District. The map I sent displays the three towns in this district: Cheer, Linger, and Grace. I know a great deal about them because the King appointed me Cheer District governor. Each district has an appointed governor whose job is simply to assist the city managers and citizens in making decisions that benefit their district and the Kingdom as a whole. I don't have a difficult job because our residents are agreeable, quite creative, and have a desire only to please their King. If they reach an impasse on something (a building project, a new road, an event), they'll consult with me. If I lack wisdom, I just ask the King, who will lead me to answers. We are all working for the same goal . . . to please the King.

Cheer is the largest city in the district. It's considered the administrative center for the district. Because there is a footpath around Lake Cheer, I can walk there quite easily to attend meetings or events. I can do the same to travel to Grace, the smallest of the three towns in the district. And of course, I can walk around the lake to Linger, which has a population midway between Grace and Cheer. I can even see Linger from Willow Bay.

Let's start with Cheer. It's a quaint city with a beautiful village green and streets lined with stone homes with leaded glass windows. A stream runs through a tree-lined town center that sweeps past an old stone mill that paddles the water as it makes its way into Lake Cheer. The townspeople are so cooperative and convivial. It's a town with a small library, shops, a town hall, and two pubs.

Grace, on the other hand, is a village half the size of Cheer. It's a town that is somewhat terraced from a smallish mountain on its far side. Gently sloping toward the lake, the town has an amphitheater nestled on the side of the mountain and has views all the way to Lake Cheer. The residents are known for their intellectual pursuits. They love to gather and discuss. People from all over come to hear speakers and watch performers in the amphitheater. I especially enjoy hearing the Proclaimers who come to speak. More on them later.

Linger is a most unique town. It's a crossroads town on the way to somewhere else. Many people consider visiting the town a delight on their way to the Great City. It's a bit of what we might have once called a "tourist town." Some might even say it's like Vanity Fair but without the vanity. The residents are joyful, humble, fun-loving, and curious about all things. What goes on there is hard to explain, but it's certainly entertaining. There's always an open market where artisans bring their items. Many enjoy the street choirs and talent shows, the pub ceilidh, unusual foods, and even the exciting rides. If I want to take a direct route from Willow Bay to Linger, I simply walk across the lake. (Yep, when we see Him, we will be like Him.)

Well, that's all for this letter. I will attempt to describe more of the larger Kingdom in my next writing.

Your friend forever,

Anne

Great is the Lord, and greatly to be praised, In the city of our God, His holy mountain.
—Psalm 48:1

My Dear Friend,

Another Sunday, another letter from me!

Since the last letter, you and I have finally met on your home turf in New Italy. Though I enjoyed passing through the other towns in your district (Peace, Joy, Tranquility, and Laughter), I am most impressed with your town of Divine. The rolling hills of vineyards, gorgeous and colorful marble buildings, art museum, and city plaza are exquisite. You are quite the tour guide too.

How much you've learned about your town and district! However, I wasn't surprised that everyone there seemed to know you because of your specific talent. I won't go into that here because you asked me not to tell your past self. It's something you'll just have to look forward to. In any case, we planned for you to visit me at Willow Bay upon your next trip to see your earthly mother in New Ireland. (You were blessed to have such a godly mom, who told you about the King from your childhood. I remember her well and mourned her passing those few years before I, too, passed through death to life.)

So you're probably wanting to know more about the Kingdom and our King. I'm delighted to tell you all that I am permitted to reveal.

King Jesus can be found on His throne in the Great City. He rules and reigns in the glory of this bejeweled and heavenly New Jerusalem, which glows from all vistas with the light that is the Father who dwells now in this New Earth. And unlike rulers on the old earth, He isn't a tyrant. He never oppresses. He only uplifts, encourages, and loves us.

Though there are "priests" who dwell in the Great City, there's no sacrificing going on there. The One Final Sacrifice, the Eternal Temple, sits on the throne most of the time. Occasionally, He travels, sometimes alone and sometimes with hosts of people and angels. (I've even heard of Him being present in multiple locations from time to time.)

There are no street signs, billboards, or anything else that would distract from the beauty of the city. Truth is, none of those items are found anywhere on New Earth—only the occasional small guideposts that simply point to Zion. It's impossible to get lost on New Earth because its center draws everyone. Besides, unless we choose to travel on foot, the way we travel often means leaving the "driving" to someone or something else. (Nope, no vehicles that typified the old earth here.)

The King's glittering throne of gold is nestled under a stunning courtyard overhang. The walls of that courtyard are covered in waterfalls of vines, flowers, fruit, and scented plants that you've never seen before. I hear that most of those plants are exclusive to the King's courtyard and were gathered from the Garden of Eden. I assume they are some of His favorite things.

There are two troughs on either side of the throne, through which clear living water flows out from the courtyard toward the street in front of the temple. (The water converges at the street and makes its way east, out of the city, like an ever-widening river.) One approaches the King down the wide center aisle made of clear stone pavers (think diamonds without facets), which allow you to see water flowing underneath. And He can see everyone before Him, all the way to the street. That's important because there are regular parades on that street. I'll describe those next time I write.

On both sides of the waterways are long tables covered in white linens and place settings for thousands. Those are for the Marriage Supper of the Lamb, and the tables are always full. Angels attend to the dining guests and continuously prepare for the next wave of visitors. One just doesn't come to the Great City without enjoying the feast. You guessed it—it's not a one-time event. It's an eternal feast. Oh, and feasters are always thrilled when the King ditches the train of His robe and comes down from His courtyard to personally speak (and sometimes eat) with them.

The rest of the Kingdom (outside the Great City) is expansive, beautiful, pristine, and inviting. Personally, I have no desires that this New Earth can't fulfill. Now, I understand that there are people here who are given to exploration. I don't know how the King fulfills their desires, but I certainly wouldn't be surprised to learn that they traverse the heavens which may be filled with things that delight those people. He fulfills the desires of our hearts because our hearts are now in unison with His. Oh, and there are no shadows here, literally and figuratively.

All for now. I've got to make a trip to the Great City to be in the follow-on crowd at a parade involving a neighbor of mine. I'll tell you all about it when I write next time.

Your friend forever,

And the Scripture was fulfilled which says, "And Abraham believed God, and it was reckoned to him as righteousness," and he was called the friend of God.

—James 2:23

My Dear Friend,

This Sunday, I thought you might want to hear about gatherings here on New Earth. I'll start with the most interesting of those. As you might expect, it takes place in the Great City. Remember that street I told you about that runs in front of the throne? That's where it occurs regularly. Each person in the Kingdom gets a parade. Since there are so many of us, I assume these parades will be held for eternity! I haven't had mine yet, but I know people in my district who have had theirs.

Let me tell you the story of one of my neighbors and her parade. Her name was Lily on the old earth—a flower symbolizing innocence, purity, and beauty. She is a raven-haired beauty. Well, she told me that a Messenger arrived one day at her home with a box. When she opened the box, she found a stunning ice-blue ball gown, matching slippers, a tiara, and gloves. The gift came with a note . . . from the King. It was His formal invitation for her to be honored in a parade before the throne. All she had to do was wear the gorgeous attire (which she can keep forever and wear whenever she chooses) and be escorted by angels that walked alongside her chariot driven by a handsome dapple stallion. She told me the whole event was spectacular and even included something akin to fireworks in the old world. Apparently, the stallion stopped just once along the road—in front of the King's courtyard. She was able to dismount, walk up that center aisle while waving to the feasters who stood up for her, and then bow before the King. She wouldn't tell me what He said to her, but her face lit up as she told me the story. I enjoyed hearing all about it. Just think—this happens regularly. He honors male and female alike, and all we can do is honor Him back! It sounds so amazing and personal. That's so like our Majesty.

Of course, we enjoy many common gatherings: in pubs, in private homes, in halls, in courtyards, on moorlands, in forests, in pavilions, and so on. Gatherings can be large (such as tens of thousands who attend a coliseum event) or small (such as when I meet my closest friend for a lakeside picnic). Even angels attend some events, but more about them later.

Personally, seeing gatherings in progress warms my heart. I've witnessed earthly family reunions on village greens, two close friends walking through woodlands without a word between them, and even annunciation events that I've been invited to attend in my official capacity as the district governor. The lasting and transparent relationships and friendships we longed for in the old world become reality here. None are excluded; new ones are developing all the time. They transcend previous cultures, generations, and languages, and no relationship falls short or disappoints. And here we never have sad goodbyes because we can always reunite.

All of this is possible because of the love that flows from the King throughout the Kingdom and its inhabitants. It's also because our first and dearest friend is the King. He never tires of us, is never distant or angry, and has never forsaken us. Like the scriptures proclaim: His steadfast love endures forever! This may be the most important thing you learn from these letters.

Now if I know you (and I do—then and now), you want to know more about those angels. Once I find out how much I can reveal about them, I'll hit that subject in my next letter.

Your friend forever,

Bless the Lord, you His angels, Mighty in strength, who perform
His word, Obeying the voice of His word!

—Psalm 103:20

My Dear Friend,

This letter is an attempt to describe something that was often written about on the old earth. Angels are unique creations. They are not like us in anything other than the fact that they walk upright. Let's review what you already know: they are created beings, their purpose is to serve the Godhead, they have great powers, and there are legions of them. Of course, we read about them making appearances in the Old and New Testaments. Back then, some people even mistook the Captain of the Host of the Lord (King Jesus) for an angel.

On New Earth, angels walk among us. We've had a long time to get to know them, yet they almost seem to fade into the background here. These are the two-thirds of all angels who stood resolutely with their Creator through all time. (The other third is in the lake of fire that burns eternally, so we have no fear of them, their "master," or those who chose to hate, ignore, or otherwise rebel against the King.)

I'm not permitted to reveal everything I know about these creatures, but here's what I can tell you: they have proportionate bodies, come in various heights (generally between four and ten feet), appear to be an all-male army for the Lord, and are structured and ranked. They consider us to be superior because the King died for us, yet they are superior to us in strength and power. Like us, each angel is unique in facial features, skin tone, hair color, eye color, talents, skills, abilities, and the like. They seem to thrive on honor, duty, and their raison d'être. We can befriend them, but it's difficult to build a relationship with them because of the demands of their work. They are by nature kind, deferential, and formal. One of my angel friends is assigned to New Antarctica. The poles are green, lush, and full of life. I can't speak to the science of New Earth and New Heaven; let's just say that there's much to learn here. Take it from scripture: nothing is impossible for the Author of science and Creator of all the planets. My angel buddy is responsible for an underground transportation system there. As we became better acquainted, I could tell he was itching to show me New Antarctica, so I asked for the tour. He was happy to show me around. Though there aren't a ton of inhabitants there, it teems with animal and plant life. The biggest city there is called Sanctuary, and it certainly is that.

Most of the angel troops live in the Great City, though some are assigned to other outposts and places unknown to me. They are dispatched from the Great City as needed to perform a myriad of duties. Frankly, the majority of them serve us as their service to their Master. However, some are specifically assigned to Him. And, of course, they all worship and adore the Great I Am.

Their leader, Michael, is a most impressive specimen of the angel "race." I speculate that he may have additional and greater power than all those under his command, though I don't know for sure. There are many things I don't know or understand about them, but it seems the King prefers to retain some mystery around angels. Still, we don't have the inordinate fascination with them the way believers and nonbelievers on the old earth had. They are important to us but seem more a part of the ecosystem of this world than anything else.

Your friend forever,

P.S. Yes, all those named in the Lamb's Book of Life had and have "guardian angels" (not the name they use). I still can't pronounce the name of mine!

God made the beasts of the earth after their kind, and the cattle after their kind, and everything that creeps on the ground after its kind; and God saw that it was good.

—Genesis 1:25

My Dear Friend,

Something tells me this will be the letter you find the most interesting. I recall our shared love of animals so very well, given that we met at an obedience class for our puppies. Today I want to share what I can about the animals here on New Earth.

There are animals here—some you will recognize, and some will be new to you unless you saw them in a zoo. There are even new additions to the animals, specific to New Earth. I used to think the Millennial Kingdom animals were as good as it got, but I was wrong. (The Creator King has never stopped creating.) There's no need for zoos because the animals aren't dangerous and roam free. They don't harm other creatures, and they seem to be intensely curious about each other. It's a precious thing to behold several deer bounding by to catch up to a bear or to witness a valiant (a new animal) running alongside a cheetah only to stop suddenly to rest together under a tree. The animals love to play with us and with each other.

The King does allow us to reunite with those animals we had on the old earth who were particularly special to us. However, sometimes they don't always come back to us in the same form. You'll know your animal because you will recognize their spirit and nature. That's the constant, though any negative traits (piddling out of fear when you approach them, running away, allergies, recalcitrance) are gone.

I am not at liberty to tell you about your "animal situation" here in the Kingdom, but I can tell you about mine. As you may recall, I had a few dogs, cats, and horses through the years on the old earth. I cared for them all, but you also know that two dogs and a horse were quite special to my heart. I loved the spirits of Pal (my horse) and my two dogs, Sweetums and Bosco. Well, the King has returned them all to me in ways I never expected.

Pal is my beautiful black-and-white draft horse. You may remember Pal as large, docile, and handsome. He's all that but now takes the form of a winged horse. He hangs around Willow Bay looking handsome but is always ready to carry me to wherever I might want to go, either by land or in the air. It's positively enchanting to have such a beast.

Bosco (that lovable tricolor mutt in our puppy class) has returned to me just as he was in his former life: a wonderful sidekick who lives at Willow Bay and wants to engage with every visitor. He has a glorious coat and bright eyes, which were once almost blind, and is even more friendly, agile, and obedient than he used to be—if that's possible.

Sweetums (with whom I had the greatest connection) was a large, strong, beautiful, alert, and yet timid dog. Here she cannot be contained because she's returned to me as a dragon. She's twice the size and weight that she was on the old earth, even stronger, just as beautiful and calm, but now courageous. She's still the same sweet spirit wrapped in a caramel-colored coat of short, soft fur, but her head reaches almost to my chest. Oh, and she can fly. Her wings fold down over her sides but shoot straight up when she's ready to fly. She knows no boundaries as one can find her almost anywhere in the district. However, if I sound our special call, she's at my side momentarily. There are other dragons here, but none quite like her.

The various animals (in the forests, mountains, dales, and towns) are made up of those that "belong to" their owners and those that are simply roaming free. All are tame and approachable. They do not kill and are not killed. Gone are their former instincts for procreation, fight-or-flight, separation anxiety, or barking at everything and anything. None of that is needed here.

I recall that you loved your dog but also always had at least one cat. There is a gal in Linger (a real cat lover) who has a miniature jaguar; it's so beautiful. (He apparently likes to "Son bathe" almost as much as Sweetums does.) Personally, I am most impressed by the lions here. They are larger than those on the old earth and so regal in their appearance. They seem to have a special relationship with their Creator. Perhaps they are his favorite animals. I should ask Him sometime.

Each land, water, and air animal is unique in personality, color, size, and type, but all have one thing in common: when they see the King, they bow. (Ever seen an owl bow?) Animals are among the most grateful creations on New Earth because they knew no sin (other than the effects of sin in the old world) and still know no sin while also being perfected. I'm not making that up. It's something the King told me when He personally delivered my animals to me at Willow Bay. Don't get me wrong, we are certainly grateful beings too. But we seemed to be exclusively the most joyful beings in the Kingdom. Perhaps it's because we are so happy with all His good gifts to us. Animals are just one of those many gifts. You're going to love it.

Your friend forever,

Anne

P.S. There is a magnificent animal that dwells in Lake Cheer. It is like nothing you have ever seen or could imagine.

Now the whole earth used the same language and
the same words.
—Genesis 11:1

My Dear Friend,

Since my last letter, the future you has come to visit me at Willow Bay and subsequently traveled on to New Ireland to visit your earthly mom. What a wonderful time we had. I thoroughly enjoyed touring Linger and Grace together. But the absolute best part was our fireside discussions of these letters and how each one of them served to increase your faith and anticipation of eternity while on the old earth.

In this letter, I want to explain a small but significant detail about this place: we speak the same language throughout the Kingdom. I don't know that you'll find that unexpected since the divergence in language was a curse for man's hubris from ancient days. Oh, I know that earthly languages were interesting, but we were designed for understanding and unity rather than confusion, division, and misunderstanding.

I'm not at liberty to elaborate on the Kingdom's sole tongue, but I will say that it's one of the most unifying aspects of our home. Like languages of old, it evolves over time with new discoveries but there is no room for separate or alternative meanings than those assigned by the design of the language. It's a very expansive, beautiful, and flexible language, and it allows for precise meaning. Being able to express all that you want to express is incredibly freeing.

Your friend forever,

P.S. Before I hand this letter over to a Messenger, it dawns on me that I've not yet addressed what seems so fundamental. It's a matter that we just take for granted in our glorified bodies. I guess that's why it didn't occur to me to mention it earlier. That is this: Everyone here is in their prime—healthy, strong, and undeterred by former physical constraints. If we want to walk across the entirety of New Earth, we have the ability to do that without fatigue, fear, cold, heat, pain, injury, hunger, or weakness. No one who was disabled, diseased, or disfigured on the old earth is now suffering those maladies. Those who then needed constant care can now help others at will. The once mentally limited are no longer restricted in acuity or by cognitive obstruction. They learn, teach, run, jump, create, work, and reason like everyone else because all of us are made new.

Then God said, "Let the earth sprout vegetation: plants yielding seed, and fruit trees on the earth bearing fruit after their kind with seed in them"; and it was so.

—Genesis 1:11

My Dear Friend,

Okay, let's talk vegetation. You knew I just had to write about this since I was a gardener in the old world. I probably shouldn't be writing on this particular subject until I make my journey to the Garden of Eden, but I'll tell you all about that trip when I make it. Admittedly, vegetation wasn't really your thing, but I thought you should know a bit about the plants in this new world.

Like everything else here, sustaining and renewing life and beauty is the regular order. Things don't need to die in order for life to continue. I can't really talk about how that's done, but a key factor is light.

In the old world, everything lived in the light of the sun. Without it, plants could not have germinated, grown, or reproduced. The original Creation was deemed "good" by the Three in One, and it was. His original systems involving sunlight, clouds, ozone, rain, elements, and the like were beyond brilliant. But on New Earth, all things are sustained by His light. It's not simply that there is no darkness, but things don't live by sunlight; they are actually filled with light. This is such a difficult thing to explain, so let me give you an example that I can relate to. I know you will too.

Remember how on the old earth I had a huge flower garden (in addition to a food garden)? What I loved growing the most were roses. That rose garden was my pride and joy, but it was also a regular reminder of the fall of mankind. Things in the Garden of Eden were free of weeds, pests, blight, and input imbalances (water, air, nitrogen, potassium, and so on). After the fall, all those perils became the backbreaking work of Adam because the old creation was under a curse. He and Eve were cast out of the Garden and destined to toil in an endless cycle to meet their basic needs. As with my rose garden, their work was a constant battle against the forces that would spoil, eat, and even kill plantings.

Now remember when we would stroll through my roses together; we'd always find something that caught our eyes. A perfect form, a delightful red, a bud of beauty, a massive spray, or even a scent to die for. Among those items were also the telltale evidence of fungal disease, drooping blooms on too-lax canes, or the dreaded rabbit damage on young plants. None of those afflictions exist here because each plant has what it needs from within and below (because living water is underground and doesn't need to fall from the sky). Each plant sustains its perfection indefinitely. You can harvest the blooms, and more perfection will appear in short order.

I do keep a small rose garden at my cottage on Willow Bay. The flowers are not just outstanding in substance and appearance, lush, prolific, and everblooming, but they come in colors that didn't exist on the old earth. They also emanate light from the inside out, which means their colors can be different from any angle on the same plant. Of course, all this potential is connected to our enhanced senses as well—some of which I'll write about another time.

Words cannot express how spectacular our plants are, and only minimal tending (for enjoyment) is required. The beauty is inexpressible. There you have it. I hope I didn't bore you with all this. I find it thrilling, and I know you will, too, upon arrival.

Your friend forever,

Proclaim good tidings of His salvation from day to day.
—I Chronicles 16:23b

My Dear Friend,

Happy Sunday! This is the day the Lord has made; rejoice and be glad in it!

This letter's subject triggered my greeting. I want to tell you about another thing that occurs here that I find absolutely delightful. Whenever I get the chance, I find my way into hearing range of a Proclaimer. What's a Proclaimer, you ask? It's someone who was called to proclaim the Gospel on the old earth and was so effective that the King never released the individual from their calling. It is their "work" here, yet they gladly do it with fervor and joy.

Remember I told you the town of Grace here in the Cheer District has an amphitheater? Well, Proclaimers often visit such places, and the people flock to hear them. They may preach for any length of time, and no one tires of them. Partly because of the vibrancy of the Gospel, which we still love to hear, and partly due to the Proclaimers' delivery. They are all different in style, but each one can bring people to their feet in worship of the King.

I mention amphitheaters, but Proclaimers can be found anywhere. They might be preaching in a pub, on the street, in the forest, in the Great City, or anywhere people gather in small or large groups to hear them. Once I was walking with Bosco along the banks of Lake Cheer when we happened upon a small group of travelers sitting under the canopy of a huge willow tree. I slipped through the hanging branches into the "hall" that the tree created. I sat down, and Bosco curled up next to me.

This particular Proclaimer was going deeper and deeper into the story of the woman at the well. Layer upon layer of meaning was exposed in his talk. He helped us relive the Gospel in the hearing, receiving, and believing in the Messiah among the Samaritan people as a result of what the woman told them. When he was done, the small crowd rose to their feet and began dancing and jumping for joy. I couldn't help but join them.

As the Proclaimer was preparing to depart for his next destination, one of the women in the crowd stepped forward to embrace him. She then turned to the small crowd and said, "I am that woman, and I am here today because the King gave me living water!" Well, as you can imagine, we all started worshiping in spirit and truth again, with even more joy and exuberance. Even Bosco was jumping and barking in sheer joy.

We love our Proclaimers here. Though they may not have been so thoroughly embraced on the old earth, we count them as very special indeed. I've heard from those who were unknown in their calling and those who you would recognize immediately. I never pass up an opportunity to hear from Simeon, Henry, Wesley, Sunday, Spurgeon, Tozer, Sproul, Graham, or any of the apostles. Yet the Proclaimers who served in lowly and quiet places are just as apt to stir you to new heights of joy in Him.

Your friend forever,

So then you are no longer strangers and aliens, but you are
fellow citizens with the saints, and are of God's household.
—Ephesians 2:19

My Dear Friend,

In one of my first letters to you, I tried to draw a picture of my home base here on New Earth. I told you about my cottage, and now you know we all have homes in this, our new and final home.

Home is a word that stirred all kinds of emotions in me when I was on the old earth. As a young girl, my family moved many times, but my mother always made for us a good and tidy home. At an early age, I was already dreaming of having my own home. If given a large box, I'd make it into a playhouse. My siblings and I would get blankets and drape them over the dining table to create a "home" underneath. Neighbor boys would create "forts" out of timber and stone. As I moved into adolescence, I thought perhaps I should become an architect because I loved making drawings of floor plans. I'd daydream about where those homes would be built and how they should be furnished. One sleek, long-roofed single-story home would be in the desert of Central America. My next creation would be a two-story house filled with large floor-to-ceiling windows and was to be found in the forested parts of North America. Oh, how I longed for a home of my own.

I'm pretty sure all those longings were set in us because we were made to desire our forever home, where we would live in the light of our Creator. His Spirit would indwell us, but we longed to be where He was, even if we didn't yet understand that longing. And since we're made in His image, it stands to reason that home is important to Him as well. Nothing has made that fact clearer to me than seeing New Earth. This is the pinnacle of His home design. The first one was the Garden of Eden, which was perfect in general. This place is perfect in the specific because He had each individual in mind as He created it. Just think, the Father gave us to Him, and He, in turn, desired to make each of us at home here with Him.

Okay, I guess that was a long and winding introduction to a simple message: each of our homes within this Home of New Earth was designed and built by the Word of the King. Because He knows us better than we know ourselves, because He knows all our needs, because He knows our desires, because He knows what delights us, and because He hears us before we even open our mouths. He spared nothing to bring us to eternal bliss.

Additionally, we have no striving, comparing, or loss of contentment in our home. We didn't buy them. We don't have debt because of them. They aren't in need of repairs. They lack nothing. And we have no need for multiple homes because everyone opens their home to visitors, strangers, and travelers. Our homes are simply a highly individualized gift from the King.

So how does all that translate into what exists here? That boy who built the fort from wood and stone has his cabin in the woods, and he loves it. The once homeless and drug-addled man who ventured into a shelter only to meet Christ now lives in his A-frame on the shores of his favorite lake, and he loves it. The woman who lost her cherished chalet to a fire has had it restored to even higher beauty in the mountains overlooking a lush valley and river below. She loves it. The orphan who grew up in institutions with nothing to call her own now abides in her Mediterranean villa perched on the side of a cliff overlooking a vast colored canyon, and she loves it. The adventuresome young man has his substantial and sturdy grass shack in the jungle, and he loves it. The city girl has her flat in town, and she loves it. The former cowboy loves his sprawling ranch surrounded by mountain views.

You'll find it all here. And while you might think it must be a hodgepodge—an eyesore that lacks conformity, you'd be amazed at how harmoniously it all works together. I guess that's because those drawn to certain home styles are drawn to live with others who like the same thing. I know that's true of my district. We love crofter cottages, rustic beams, timber frames, village greens, chocolate boxes, old mills, dry stone fences, arbors, leaded glass, and cobbled streets.

Each home within this Home was heart-crafted by the One who knows us thoroughly. And we love it.

Your friend forever,

Anne

No longer do I call you slaves, for the slave does not know what his master is doing; but I have called you friends, for all things that I have heard from My Father I have made known to you.
—John 15:15

My Dear Friend,

I wanted to return this week to the subject of friendships and relationships. It's a thread that is woven throughout the Kingdom and ties us all together.

I have many friends here in the Cheer District but also friends in other lands. It seems like I am constantly meeting and making new friends. One can hardly go to an event or shop without meeting a stranger who is now known to you. The wonderful thing about friendships here is that there is no "station in life," generation, era, sex, rank, legacy, denomination, ethnicity, country of origin, language, or anything else that would preclude someone from friendship. In other words, everyone is approachable, and everyone is open to friendship. And like-mindedness isn't a criterion anymore because we share the mind of Christ. That isn't a "hive" mentality; it's simply the basis upon which we now appreciate the diversity and differences that He created in us.

Here's a story for you. When I first arrived here, I visited a pub in Cheer for the first time. Two men were sitting in chairs in the corner of the room next to the open fireplace. When I walked in alone, one of the two men motioned to me to approach them. As one pulled up a chair for me, the other exclaimed, "No one should sit alone in this warm and inviting place!" I thanked them but indicated that I didn't want to interrupt their conversation. They would have nothing of that and simply brought me into their discussion of early Christian art and architecture. This is a subject I knew very little about and was eager to learn more. (There's no end to learning here.) I indicated that I probably couldn't contribute much but could listen well.

The discussion was brilliant, lively, and so informative to all of us. By the end of the hour, I realized I hadn't even tried the well-known delicacy of this establishment. The conversation was just that engrossing, and these men were so endearing, humble, intelligent, and witty. Apparently, these guys had met and become fast friends in Paradise, and here on New Earth, they meet up often over tea to discuss a variety of subjects.

As we departed the pub as a threesome, I learned we were each going in different directions. It seemed a shame to have to part ways, so I asked for their names and where I was most likely to find them again. I was stunned to learn that I had been engaging with Clive Staples Lewis in deep conversation with Constantine the Great.

And what about our earthly familial relations? Though I am not permitted to say much about your family members of the old earth, I will try to shed light on this matter in general.

We are all one family here, but each of us has old-earth family here as well. To be sure, there are people in the Kingdom who were the only believers in their first family. Having said that, even they have gotten to know the family members in their past generations who were believers. In fact, I can't tell you how many people have told me that their aunt, grandmother, cousin, or great-uncle prayed for their salvation when there may have been no one else to do so. Our Great God heard and honored such prayers.

Does this mean we are aware of lost loved ones? We are. However, we have all assurance from the King that those lost had every opportunity to respond to Him. So the question from old earth becomes: can you trust Him with your family members? Ultimately, is there really anyone else who can be trusted with the souls of men? The nonbeliever thought he was the captain of his own destiny, the end of things, the decider. He bought those lies from the world, the Enemy of God, and even his own feeble and arrogant mind. And I can confirm to you that even though they had to admit that Jesus Christ is Lord, the lost have not changed their minds; they still hate Him without regret. They weep only for themselves; they wail over their condition, but they gnash their teeth with contempt for God and His Christ.

Our reunions with relatives from old earth are quite sweet—particularly between parents and their children. I especially love to hear the stories of those who lost a child at or before birth (a very common occurrence before what we used to call "modern medicine"). It's a reunion of those who can now have a life together and become fast friends. Conversely, I've met people who survived their own mother's death upon their delivery into the old world. Now they can embrace and know each other forever! During the time of the Millennial Kingdom, I met most of my relatives from eons past—all the way back to the very first believer in our family. (As a pagan adrift in a sea of fear, animism, and the occultic practices of his tribe on the European continent, he was the first to respond to the Gospel delivered by a traveler from a faraway land.)

Yes, the reunions and the new relationships are endless and spectacularly joyous.

Your friend forever,

For all of you who were baptized into Christ
have clothed yourselves with Christ.
—Galatians 3:27

My Dear Friend,

Have you wondered what we wear, if anything? No, it's not a nudist camp, and just because Adam and Eve were created as unclothed beings, doesn't mean we've returned to that state here!

Clothing is truly an art form on New Earth. It's not my gift, but many here design and create incredible items for the rest of us to wear. And, like everything else, we buy without money. I'm not saying our closets are full, but I love to get and give unique clothing items.

Most of my time is spent wearing a one-piece undergarment with something over that such as a tunic, pants, a skirt, or a jumper-style garment. Some people here like to wear bright colors and fancy clothes, but I tend to opt for more subdued colors and casual things. And no status is associated with clothing. No one thinks they must "keep up with the Joneses" by any measure.

In any case, if I know you, you'll be so relieved there isn't a required uniform. (Angels are the only exception to that.) Ever since the end of the tribulation period, we have been free to express ourselves through our attire, and nobody here would think of wearing something offensive to others.

The clothing artisans are just that. Nothing is mass-produced. Everything is custom-made and well-thought-out. Many of the artisans sew or weave some of New Earth's more unusual elements, gems, and metallics right into their designs.

Jewelry crafters, bags and carrier makers, hatmakers, and many others come up with the most unusual accessories. Of course, the various regions (where whole cultures of people made their homes on old earth) influence clothing design. For example, I'm not that big on hats, but I've admired many a turban obtained from the east. People don't travel to get clothing; it's just something you might pick up in the process of traveling.

I hope this Sunday has been a blessed one for you.

Your friend forever,

Anne

P.S. Before I write my next letter, I'm going to make that trip to the Garden of Eden.

And her wilderness He will make like Eden, and her desert like
the garden of the Lord; Joy and gladness will be found in her,
Thanksgiving and sound of a melody.
—Isaiah 51:3b

My Dear Friend,

The Garden of Eden was amazing. The whole of Heaven and Earth
are new, so the Garden is new as well. However, I was told that it
is a replication (renewal) of the home Adam and Eve lived in for
some time before the Fall. The most notable difference is that no
angel with a flaming sword guards the entryway to the Tree of Life.
We are able to walk right into the Garden and behold its splendor.

All manner of beautiful plants grow in the garden, and the
Tree of Life may be filled with any of the twelve fruits that it pro-
duces. (When I was there, it was a fruit that I'm told is something
akin to a plum that we knew on the old earth but sweeter.) And the
river that originates in New Jerusalem is divided and runs through
the garden. Thousands of travelers were in the Garden of Eden
when I was visiting. We were all in awe of its beauty because light
emanated through it from the ground up and out to the heavens.
We all felt a certain hushed reverence as we approached that tree.

Every visitor in the Garden ate from the Tree of Life—an act
that represents the healing of the nations. We all wanted to partake
in the life-giving tree, not just because it's beautiful and the fruit
is sumptuous, but because it's the greatest gift from the King. It
represents Him, and He would want everyone to taste and see that
He is good.

I know you're not that into plants, so I won't describe the flora that I've never seen before or anywhere else since, but I do have to tell you about what happened as I was departing.

I had traveled to the garden on Pal's wings because I wanted to get there and back home quickly. Leaving Pal outside the Garden to wait, I returned to find a woman talking sweetly to him and burying her face in his glorious mane. I remember thinking that this has happened before because he's so beautiful and there are many animal lovers here. However, as I walked up to greet her, she turned to me and asked if he belonged to me. I answered affirmatively but was almost speechless when I beheld her beauty. All women are beautiful here, but I don't think I've ever seen one so lovely as this woman. Her flowing hair was light brown and almost reached to the back of her knees. Her facial features were completely symmetrical, her skin flawless, and her figure ideally womanly.

I told her my name, and she told me hers. She was Eve in her prime! In a flash, it dawned on me just how close to perfection our earthly parents were, even years after the Fall. No wonder they lived for hundreds of years, while those of us who lived closer to the end of the old earth's age had a shorter lifespan due to millennia of decay, decline, and the effects of sin.

We gathered Pal, and she invited me into her home nearby. We spent lots of time together, and I was able to learn so much from her. Of course, I invited her to visit me at Willow Bay. I think I have another best friend!

Your friend forever,

"Whether, then, you eat or drink or whatever you do, do all to the glory of God."

—I Corinthians 10:31

My Dear Friend,

When I was a little girl on old earth, I can remember my father waking me up one Sunday to get dressed for church. I was groggy and didn't want to get up. So I asked him, "Do I have to go to church?" He put his finger to his lips as if in deep thought for several seconds. Finally, he responded, "No, you get to go to church." He is such a wise man. (I love visiting with him in the Great City where he makes his home.)

I think that's the same sentiment we have here about work. While you might ask if we *have* to go to work, we would say we are *blessed* to work. I suppose, like everything else on the fallen earth, the concept of work has been spoiled by sin.

On the old earth, work often took the form of endless repetition, it lacked creativity, it was routinized such that we didn't really have to apply ourselves, and it became drudgery or worse—meaningless. Not everyone disliked their work, but the majority were living for the weekend or retirement. And even those who found fulfillment in their work would acknowledge aspects of it that they hated. Work was often viewed as a means to an end. Some even spent a lifetime avoiding work. Our bodies would bend and eventually break under physical and mental strain. And in many places on old earth, labor was coerced, deadly, and never rewarded. None of that is so here because New Earth makes the crooked paths straight. Work has been restored to worth because the Master is worthy.

I have already told you about my own work. In my former life, I had faint gifts of planning, administration, and serving. The King chose to enhance and continue those gifts on New Earth. I thoroughly enjoy assisting in the building of the Kingdom. That little girl who loved to design homes is now helping to design communities. In my mind, it's the perfect melding of architecture and people. It hardly seems like work because we don't battle the former constraints of time, quality, and resources. Those are limitless here.

People here perform all kinds of work they enjoy, and they have been gifted accordingly. I already told you about Proclaimers, artisans, clothiers, shopkeepers, and gardeners. Most have completely different vocations on New Earth than they did on old earth. For example, physicians are no longer needed. The healer of old has become a master woodworker or stonemason. Those who once slaughtered animals as products now tend them. The former soldier has become an art museum docent, and the childcare worker is now free to create the art housed in that museum. The dentist is now creating beautiful maps of New Earth. And someone must organize those parades, after all.

To be sure, writers still write, teachers still teach, painters still paint, and landscapers still design and install gardens. But regardless of the type of work we do here, we do it all to the glory of the King and for the benefit of His people.

Your friend forever,

Whatever you do, do your work heartily, as for the Lord
rather than for men.
—Colossians 3:23

My Dear Friend,

One of the things I used to hear in the old world was people musing on heaven being a boring place. I guess they assumed we'd be angels sitting on clouds (which they never do, by the way), playing harps for the rest of eternity. Those thoughts were from the Evil One who always attempted to paint God as a dud. This letter is intended to try to express just how *not* boring this place really is.

So my last letter talked about work. Now we'll dive into play, entertainment, fun, recreation . . . whatever you want to call it. Here we just think of it as another form of worship. (The Evil One used *worship* to limit people's understanding of the act, more often than not, to just singing hymns.) Remember, we do all things to His glory and in the light of that glory.

What does that worship look like? It may involve enjoying those rides at Linger or lawn bowling on the village green in Cheer. Whatever you consider fun. So, while I might not enjoy the game of Bobble, there are entire leagues across this world that play. My favorite forms of entertainment are live music, live theater, dance, and opera, but performances aren't everyone's cup of tea. Some people just make it a habit of attending bazaars, street fairs, or open markets. And, as I mentioned in my last letter, some people love their work so much that it's also their avocation. People who design and install gardens may find recreation in tending their own gardens. A woman from Linger, who is a chef by trade, organizes district-wide bake-offs as her hobby.

Knowing you there (and here), I'm not surprised you love to hike, with particular emphasis on finding and observing animals. That really is fun.

Besides the solo and team activities, New Earth has a myriad of events. There are regular festivals in the Great City, touring exhibits and displays, art shows, and more. We build sandcastles, airships, cakes, and trains; we perform in orchestras and traveling shows; we create new games and toys; and we put on dazzling fireworks displays. These may seem like old-earth pursuits, but I can't stress enough that they are bigger and better because of the lack of constraints. No one here says, "That can't be done." And, of course, all things are possible with God.

So much to look forward to, eh?

Your friend forever,

*And there are also many other things which Jesus did, which if
they were written in detail, I suppose that even the world itself
would not contain the books that would be written.*
—John 21:25

My Dear Friend,

Are there books here? You bet there are!

In fact, we have many libraries around New Earth, but the largest is a project completed some time ago. It's located in New France, and the building itself is fifty thousand square meters or just under six hundred thousand square feet. (I had to translate that for you because we use cubits for measurement here.) It's thirty levels, and ten of those are below ground. Some of those floors are amazing feats of engineering because they house displays like aquariums and even a replica of the Lamb's Book of Life with "living pictures" of each Kingdom inhabitant. It's so big I wouldn't be surprised if everyone in the surrounding districts worked there.

The building exterior is a beautiful shell-and-coral-colored granite exterior. It gleams in the light of Christ. The reading room floor has recumbent chairs. You can just lay back, relax, and read to your heart's content. Companion animals are allowed in too. Sweetums loves the place. And who doesn't want to read with their small dragon curled up nearby?

Literacy levels are exceedingly high coming out of the work done during the Millennial Kingdom period to bring people up to those levels. Our libraries are a great place to meet bibliophiles, authors, poets, historians, scientists, and everyday people who love to explore and learn. And while the reading area is quiet, there are plenty of snugs where conversations, meetings, and educational sessions can take place.

Enough about libraries. Let's talk about what we read here. Needless to say, the Word of God is the most popular. (The Great City has a massive scriptorium.) After that, the great works of antiquity and more modern eras are consumed. Lastly, people are still writing. My brother is a poet, and I have a book of his work on my shelf at home. Similarly, many people enjoy going to readings of poetry and books, and we have book clubs. Gone are the writings of sinful man: the gratuitously creepy, bloody, ugly, lustful, frightening, vile, and horrible. But then, most writers of such things from the old earth aren't here either.

Well, I don't have many more opportunities to write to you. So many subjects, and so little time.

Your friend forever,

Anne

P.S. Solomon was just being a "wise guy" when he dissed the making and studying of many books. He is no longer feeling jaded like he was on old earth where there was nothing new under the sun. Here, everything is new under the Son!

By common confession, great is the mystery of godliness: He who was revealed in the flesh, Was vindicated in the Spirit, Seen by angels, Proclaimed among the nations, Believed on in the world, Taken up in glory.
—I Timothy 3:16

My Dear Friend,

This may be the hardest of all the letters to write. In part due to my restrictions, but also because the subject is almost inexpressible.

On old earth, I once had a pastor who used to say, "We live in an enchanted world." I'd never heard anyone put it that way, though I understood (and experienced) what he meant. It was true then because the unseen world was active, and the seen world was beautiful to behold if you let yourself contemplate it rather than take it for granted. However, New Earth is enchantment on steroids. (Have you ever seen a giraffe bow before its Maker?)

There may be things I've already described to you that you find enchanting. I hope so. But let me attempt to bring you a little closer to that enchantment.

Not that long ago a man came running up to me after a concert in Grace. He said he'd been looking for me for quite some time and thought he might find me here. After he collected himself, I asked him how I could help. He said, "You already helped. I just came to thank you for it. When I was in my twenties on old earth, I was involved in a serious auto accident. You drove by the accident well after the police and ambulance had been called. You might remember seeing the EMTs hovering over me on the hot pavement that day. Because years earlier you had made a promise to God to pray for those involved whenever you came upon an accident or heard a siren, you began praying and did so all the way to your office that day. You prayed for me to be healed physically and spiritually. You prayed that what Satan meant for evil, God would use for good. That was me, and I just had to find you and thank you for that brief act of obedience. I am here because of His mercy, but you played an important role." That's enchantment.

As I mentioned before, a large beast lives in Lake Cheer. No, it's not Nessy, but it is quite beautiful. It is dark blue with large scales the size of dinner plates. Occasionally, it surfaces and breathes fire toward the heavens. Like all other creatures here, it's never harmed anyone and appears to be quite shy. Is that enchanting enough? Well, one day I was down on Willow Bay's beach by the lake just staring off toward Linger when the beast (which we affectionately call Clarabelle) surfaced and approached me. When she neared my shore, I could see her feet walking under the shallow water as her large body was increasingly exposed. I wasn't frightened, but I did wonder what this encounter might mean, so I decided to sit down on the sand. Within moments, Clarabelle was fully out of the water, and I could see and hear her shiny clacking scales, her water wings, her big head with tiny ears, and her large claws. She made her way toward me and turned toward the lake to sit her big self down next to me. I looked into her large dark eyes and could tell immediately she wanted attention, so I hugged as much of her as I could for as long as I could. I don't think she was created to be out of the water for very long, so I released her, and she lumbered back into the lake. But before she submerged, she turned back to look at me again. I swear she winked. That's enchantment.

I once attended a gathering in the Great City to honor King David. He danced before the Lord. Everyone did. That's enchantment.

There are angels here who do nothing but sing over the Great City. Their perpetual serenading is more than the chant of "Holy, Holy, Holy, is the Lord of hosts, the whole earth is full of His glory," although that's a favorite for all of us. They have written other songs to laud Him and even sing some of the music created by New Earth inhabitants. Their vocal range far exceeds ours.

We must listen using our enhanced auditory abilities to hear them over the normal city sounds—still, that's enchantment.

Our forests are home to "companion trees." If you search for a stand of these trees in the forest, you'll see them lined up in a row or sometimes in a circle with their branches entwined together like loving arms. When there is a breeze, their leaves hum an inviting and pleasant sound. It's positively enchanting.

I met and broke bread with Moses in his expansive tent home. He's back to tending sheep in a beautiful valley at the base of a mountain. While I was there, Isaac dropped by to chat. No, not the Old Testament Isaac . . . Isaac Newton. It was enchanting.

The Glassy Sea really does emit what looks like fire sparks. The effect is actually light reflecting and refracting from all the jewels in all the golden crowns that were placed therein. It's enchanting.

I could go on and on, but I think you get the enchantment.

Your friend forever,

Jesus said to them, "I am the bread of life; he who comes to Me will not hunger, and he who believes in Me will never thirst."
—John 6:35

My Dear Friend,

I hope you're having a wonderful Sunday. Rest and be glad in it!

I'm wondering if you've been scratching your head about the mentions in previous letters of food here on New Earth. I think some people assume that no hunger, thirst, pain, tears, or suffering means New Earth inhabitants are merely zombies walking around. That's crazy and false. Probably just another lie from that Old Deceiver.

We do have food here. It's glorious in appeal, taste, and smell. Do we have to eat because we get hungry? Nope. Do we desire to eat some of this amazing food? Yep.

Let's start with the perpetual feast, the Marriage Supper of the Lamb, in the Great City. Its tables are filled with wonderful fare, which the angels replenish regularly. We don't get a menu or have waiters. Diners take food from community platters and bowls full of savory, sweet, tangy, and earthy items. And as with most weddings, there's wine. It's some of the best food in this world. You can take as little or as much as you want. It's a real party atmosphere because you're right there with the Groom. The word *lavish* perfectly describes what's going on at this Supper.

Of course, lots of other events serve food. Most people don't keep or store food in their homes unless they plan to entertain others. That's because we don't require food. Some people enjoy preparing food, while others like to pick it up from local shops.

Wine from vintners from around the world can be had, but no one gets drunk.

Want to try manna? You can do that, but it's available only in the Great City. The King is the exclusive Creator of that food, and He makes some available to the residents to collect and provide to those who want it. It's considered a novelty. I've had it deep-fried on a stick. It melts in your mouth.

I think some of the best food can be found at town markets and fairs. Chefs come up with beautiful presentations of delectable foods. Much of it might be familiar to you (based on the place where you lived on the old earth), but there's so much more that you've never heard of or tried.

Anyway, I thought you should know that you're literally in for a real treat!

Your friend forever,

Hear, O Israel! The Lord is our God, the Lord is one!
—Deuteronomy 6:4

My Dear Friend,

I'd like to use this Sunday letter to talk about my favorite subject—the Great I Am. Recall in the book of Genesis where it says that God spoke these words: "Let Us make man in Our image." Our first introduction to Him through His Word is His pronouns *Us* and *Our*. Of course, they are a reference to the Triune God—Father, Son, and Spirit.

Here on New Earth, we no longer just hear, read, and believe. We can *see* how One superintends (Father); One speaks, orchestrates, and sustains (Son); and One executes, helps, and moves (Spirit). Remember, God dwells with us again. To see the glory of God in your midst is powerful and something we never fully grasped in the old world. Seeing in this way is a constant reminder that the transcendent God of the universe knows each one of us. His Christ would not know us if God didn't know us first. And the Spirit drew us to Him in the first place.

I'm probably preaching to the choir on all this, but I can't emphasize enough how pivotal the reality of dwelling with God is to New Earth. It's a sine qua non.

I also wanted to discuss His omnipresence because that subject has always been a bit mind-blowing. The King can be in multiple places at once. If He is needed in the Great City but also chooses to visit the home of a certain Proclaimer while also needing to give orders to a leader of the angels but is also invited to speak at a conference of the martyrs, He can do all those things at the same time. You see, He has this amazing ability to answer us even before we speak our request. And as you might expect, every word He speaks is full of wisdom, encouragement, and love because He is the exact representation of God the Father.

Well, I didn't intend to take on such a weighty subject in this letter, but there it is. I hope it's edifying to you in some way.

Your friend forever,

Anne

And not only this, but also we ourselves, having the first fruits
of the Spirit, even we ourselves groan within ourselves, waiting
eagerly for our adoption as sons, the redemption of our body.
—Romans 8:23

My Dear Friend,

Welcome, Sunday!

In this letter, I want to address something that I've swerved into in past letters but never hit head-on. People of old earth were always speculating about our physical bodies. To put it succinctly, when you see Him here, you will be like Him here.

Let's drill down on that because I want to disabuse you of any notions that we become Jesus or gods. To be like Him simply means our glorified bodies can do many of the things that His physical body can do. So what's included there? For that, you can take some cues from the Word. Remember when the risen Christ walked through material to appear inside someone's house? Remember when Mary mistook the risen Christ for being part of the landscaping crew? Remember when He told her not to cling to Him because He had not yet ascended to the Father? Those things should tell you that His physical body could do amazing things that nobody else on old earth could do. Those weren't tricks, and He wasn't employing some kind of advanced technology. He really can walk through matter. He doesn't need to shape-shift to be unrecognizable; He can veil eyes and minds so that they can't see Him for who He is. He can walk on water. He can appear and disappear.

What about our glorified bodies are enhanced from our earthly bodies? I am not permitted to tell you all things, but we don't need to eat, we don't get sick, we don't age, and we have superior senses in terms of the ones we used to have. We don't eliminate, we don't have allergies, and we don't tire. We don't even get splinters or blisters or stung by a bee. Much of our enhancement has to do with light energy, biomineralization, and other functions in our bodies, but even more has to do with the environment created for these bodies. And primarily, it has to do with the fact that all things are possible with God.

We recognize those we knew in life, and now we recognize all those we've come to know. There is also knowledge that we acquired the minute we were in His presence long ago. Those were things we needed to know in order to enter into our rest. (That's not to say we know everything, and there are many questions we ask Him even now.)

The bottom line is that we bear His name and many of His traits. We are, in fact, fitted for our new home.

Your friend forever,

Now there are varieties of gifts, but the same Spirit.
—I Corinthians 12:4

My Dear Friend,

This Sunday I'd like to cover the matter of gifts. In times past (like the one in which you receive these letters), God gave His people certain gifts. So one might have the gift of service or the gift of teaching and so on. Those were all to be used to edify the Body and glorify God. I'm certain that many believers went through life not knowing their gifts or not using them much. That was sad indeed. And we were all held accountable for our sins of omission as well as commission, although Jesus paid for all of that.

Here on New Earth, we're far past those days. We don't even have the "storehouse" of gifts anymore. That was a giant warehouse in the Millennial Kingdom that was said to house the many gifts and talents that God had in store for His people that they never prayed for or used. I never saw the warehouse myself and suspect it was only a rumor. I don't think I could have stood seeing all the things I missed out on.

On old earth, we did not have because we didn't ask. On old earth, we thought our giftedness was our own ability or a result of experience and education—such an affront to the One from whom all good gifts are given.

Now we are acutely aware of our gifts. Nobody would think of not using them for the King. Some even venture to ask for additional gifts to complement the ones they have. And He gives freely to all who ask. I specifically asked for an empathic ability, and He gave it to me in ways that exceeded my expectations.

I know a man here who asked to view the heavens (beyond the atmosphere), and it was granted to him. Over in New Spain, he manages an immense telescope that enhances our already amazing vision. He gives tours and teaches all about the new heavens. And a group of dozens in New Greece study the various gems, minerals, and elements here. Those people are amazingly gifted, and their research tells us all more about this New Creation. In turn, we rejoice more and praise the King even more because of it!

You have a very special gift, though I think I've mentioned that I can't divulge that. On New Earth, you are widely known because of your gift.

Well, I need to move along—friends are waiting on me to join them at a concert!

Your friend forever,

*The foundation stones of the city wall were adorned with every
kind of precious stone.*
—Revelation 21:19a

My Dear Friend,

Perhaps you've wondered about the gems of New Earth since they are mentioned in the Word. Well, most of them are minerals, and I must tell you that those listed in the Book are just a sampling of what we have here. In fact, it seems these were singled out because we would know them as minerals found on the old earth. So yes, we see various quartz, gold, silver, and pearls throughout the Kingdom. Because He makes all things new, there are also gems here that didn't exist on the old earth.

Let's start with the notion that the Great City has gold bars for pavers. That was just a silly notion. While a huge part of the city and her streets are gold, it's more like clear glass because gold in its purest form is transparent. There has never been and never will be another city like the Great City. It's one of those inexpressible things. Her twelve city gates (always open) are each fashioned from a single pearl. Imagine how big those oysters must have been! All this, and everything stays beautiful and pristine because our environment doesn't break down organic matter, such as pearl, and having no UV rays or pollution means no damage to the minerals.

Now you might be wondering if all this grandeur is just in New Jerusalem. Splendor was most extravagantly lavished upon that city, to be sure. However, all elements, minerals, and organics can be harvested on New Earth and used to decorate throughout the Kingdom.

There is much I can't tell you, but this place is exquisite. It is fit for the King of the Universe and His people. Old earth certainly had her beauty, but this New Earth has been resurrected to something that is most impressive. You're going to love it here. Oh wait, you already do!

Your friend forever,

Anne

P.S. I feel like I keep repeating myself about everything here that didn't exist on the old earth. I just want to make clear that nothing is lost on New Earth, but much is added, improved, renewed, extended, and enlarged. Embedded in this concept of nothing being lost is also the fact that nothing really died. Oh sure, we felt deeply the loss of our elderly parent, our beloved pet, or a land we were forced to leave. However, the loss was just a temporary separation. Had we really grasped that He held everything in His hand and lost nothing He intended to keep, we might have labored less in our pain and grief. Only on this side of eternity are we able to fully comprehend this marvelous truth. On your side of eternity, you must grab hold of it by faith, which the King supplies if you ask.

For I consider that the sufferings of this present time are not
worthy to be compared with the glory that is to be revealed to us.
—Romans 8:18

My Dear Friend,

Good Sunday morning! I can hardly believe I have only a few more opportunities to write to you. Because those opportunities are dwindling, I thought I'd use this letter to cover something that used to weigh heavy on my mind on old earth.

You see, even though we knew that this New Earth would set all things right, we wondered about how old wrongs and hurts might be dealt with. Does God just wipe away the memories when He wipes away the tears? Well, not exactly. It's a bit more like He replaced our sorrows with His joy.

So, yes, you're going to run into people here who may have hurt you during your old-earth life. You worked hard to forgive them as we are commanded to forgive. Yet, because of our old nature, we often couldn't completely let our resentment go. Perhaps you remember that coworker, someone you thought was a friend, who lied about you to others and caused dissension in the ranks as a result. I'm not permitted to tell you whether that person is here. However, I can tell you that almost everyone here has had that kind of thing happen to them. Or worse, they were the betrayer. Given that (and the fact that our King was betrayed by His own— and even by us in the old life when we didn't trust Him or we stole His glory), we also all know that we are new creations now. Never again will we betray Him or each other.

The home we have in the glorious Kingdom is our final peace and joy. We've all been through the old earth that was fallen, the

55

Millennial Kingdom, and the final silencing of Satan, his rebels, and his followers. Sin is gone for eternity. Subsequently, we see everyone who might have done us wrong with new eyes. Firstly, we're glad they ended up counted among the righteous. Secondly, those old hurts and grudges make no sense to us anymore. And lastly, we're all reconciled to God and to each other.

What about those unkind or judgmental words we spoke about a fellow believer, those theological disagreements, and the times we cut people out of our circle over a point of contention? The good news is that all those disagreements, the denominational divisions, the beef we had over what form baptism should take, the oaths we shouldn't have taken, and the like are settled. We know fully the Truth, the Way, and the Life as it was always intended from the beginning. Eve told me about life in the garden, how she and Adam walked and talked to God, and how there was never a cross word, a bad mood, a turning away, or a disagreement. Fully knowing the Truth sets us fully free. That's the way it is here in this "new garden."

Am I saying that our past sins were washed away because the Jesus we trust in paid for them? Yes, that's exactly what I'm saying. If that seems too simplistic, it's because you're still holding on to hurts. The old nature uses grudges as protection against further hurts. The old nature gives up on people (which always leads to contempt). I was certainly guilty of that and more. But here we have no threat of future hurts. And no one here would think of giving up on anyone because, despite our sins in the past, God never gave up on us. Can you see how the lack of sin and threats frees everyone to move beyond and forward?

It's not as if we aren't aware of our past hurts. And every time we see our Lord's nail-pierced hands, we are reminded that we too hurt others in the past, but we are forgiven because of His blessed sacrifice. From your vantage point, it's a matter of faith, but believe me, the sufferings of old earth aren't worth being compared with the glory that has been revealed to us here.

Lastly, let me just say, the hallmarks of New Earth are truth, beauty, peace, and joy. I have witnessed people who wronged each other on the old earth meeting up on New Earth. They are loving, forgiving, and reconciled, and the greatest sign of all that is their joy. We are constantly celebrating in joy that our old nature, our old accuser, and the old earth have passed away. Truly, all things are new.

Your friend forever,

Anne

P.S. Yes, you're going to find people here that you didn't expect to be here. Conversely, you're going to be surprised at those you assumed would be here who aren't. Tread carefully with everyone you meet knowing that He may not be finished with them. On the other hand, know that not everyone who says "Lord, Lord" is someone the Father knows.

For we are God's fellow workers; you are God's field,
God's building.
—I Cor. 3:9

My Dear Friend,

I hope this letter finds you well. It's weird not to know what season you're in, if your birthday is approaching, or even where you live at this point in your time. When I saw you last (here), we never talked about those things because we had so much to catch up on. I guess I'll just have to wish you a happy birthday and wonderful holidays all together!

Today I thought I would tackle the art of the Kingdom. There is plenty of it. I've already mentioned that New Earth has amazing artisans: blacksmiths, gem cutters, architects, sculptors, painters, fashion designers, gardeners, and so much more. Some artists even work with materials unknown on old earth.

As I mentioned in my last letter, two hallmarks of the Kingdom are truth and beauty. Unlike on the old earth where people didn't seem to link the two (hence, we got some ugly stuff they called "art"), there is so much truth in the art here. The King seems to love seeing His subjects building and creating. I guess that's because we are reflecting His strengths in doing so. After all, He created the beautiful canvas upon which we paint.

Many letters ago, I mentioned the expansive library we have in New France. That library contains many works of art to admire while you're enjoying the reading facilities. But our largest museum of art is in New Wales. I love living so close to that museum. It's huge and spectacular. It contains all kinds of paintings, statuary, lightworks, and glassworks. It also contains some of the masterpieces we knew on the old earth. I wonder what those famous artists who live on New Earth think when they see their work in the museum. I really must ask da Vinci when I meet him. (Yep, he submitted to the King in his last days on old earth. His art made here is even more favorable to the King.)

Any district can obtain some of these works to display in town. It's just a matter of sending a request for them. I have approved many of these transfers to places like Cheer. We just return the art or pass it on to another district that has requested it.

Well, that's all for now and on this subject!

Your friend forever,

Anne

For in the resurrection they neither marry
nor are given in marriage.
—Matthew 22:30a

My Dear Friend,

I'd like to address what may be a difficult subject for you. I say that because when I first met you on old earth, you were recovering from a difficult loss. I remember when we went for coffee after that puppy class, and you told me about becoming a widow just six months earlier. It became clear that the lingering pain of losing your beloved husband of six years had driven you to get a puppy to help with your loneliness. We both know a puppy won't take the place of a loving spouse, but I certainly couldn't blame you for wanting to take the edge off of being alone. I think we became fast friends that day because you shared so openly. We cried, we laughed, and we made a commitment to try to be there for each other regardless of where life took us. (I now know that you tried to get to my bedside as I lay dying on the old earth, but I was already in Paradise when you arrived. Bless you, my friend, for trying. But remember, you are blessed in this Kingdom where our friendship is restored and renewed.)

So today I wanted to address a matter that was frequently pondered and misunderstood on the old earth. That's the matter of marriage.

Marriage was created by God for inhabitants of old earth for several reasons. Firstly, God determined it was not good for man to be alone. Secondly, God knew that man would need a helper by his side. Thirdly, for procreation. Lastly, marriage was supposed to be a picture of the King and His Bride—the Church.

The scriptures clearly tell us that in our resurrection and life on New Earth men don't marry and women aren't given in marriage. But you, dear friend, had a wonderful marriage on the old earth. (In fact, you may marry again…but I'm not at liberty to confirm or deny any such thing about your future on the old earth.) Therefore, you must wonder about the blessed reunion you long for with your husband who knew the Lord and dwells with Him. As I've mentioned before, reunions are wonderful events to behold on New Earth. You can rest assured that you will see that man again. However, you won't be married to him. In fact, you aren't married to him now because death has parted you two. But your marriage on the old earth certainly lived up to the purpose of marriage that God had in mind. Steve was not alone; you were a wonderful help to him. And though you weren't able to have children, the two of you reflected how Christ loves His Bride and would die for her. In many respects, Steve did die for you (and so many others) due to his military service to our country, which led to his untimely death.

What I want to clearly say is that there is no need to mourn the loss of marriage on New Earth because it is no longer needed. Man is not alone here—we are all friends. Nobody needs a helper here because God, Christ, and His Spirit attend to our every need. Like the animals here, we have no instinct or need to have off-spring. And lastly, the Bride (the Church) is ultimately united with her Bridegroom for eternity. Every day is a wedding here—and the honeymoon never ends!

Does this mean we don't have a special place in our hearts for a former loving husband? Banish that thought! Let me use my new friend, Eve, as an example. Remember when I met her and went to her home not far from the Garden of Eden? Well, she and Adam spent hundreds of years together on the old earth, and now they both live in the Bountiful District. They can see each other whenever they wish. They fulfilled their charge to "be fruitful and multiply," and they certainly were true partners on old earth. Now they are partners of God and close friends of each other. So it will be with you and Steve.

Perhaps you're wondering about the opposite case. What about people who experienced divorce with ongoing enmity between their former partners? Well, as you might expect, that common scenario on the old earth (divorce being permitted due to the hardness of our selfish and self-indulgent hearts) plays out in different ways here on New Earth. For example, divorced couples who rejected God and His Christ were dead in their sins already and behaving as you might expect of nonbelievers. Those couples are not here because of their hatred for God. Then some couples were unequally yoked—one a believer and one not. Here on New Earth, the believer is happy in Christ. But what if the nonbeliever later (after divorcing the believer) comes to salvation in Christ? In that case, both are here, free of their past disputes, grudges, and betrayals, and rejoicing they are in the Kingdom. Hanging on to past loss, shame, or anger makes no sense to them anymore.

In short, all our affection and allegiance is to our King. Our purpose in life is (and should always have been) to glorify God and enjoy Him forever. Then what is God's purpose? To receive glory, of course! That's not because He's needy or conceited as that would be outside of His nature and character. Instead, it's because He's worthy of all glory, laud, and honor. And believe me when I say this: we are experiencing complete and total enjoyment of Him.

Well, I didn't mean to go on so but wanted to address this issue because I'm certain it has crossed your mind and probably the minds of everyone you know.

Your friend forever,

And they celebrated the feast seven days, and on the eighth day there was a solemn assembly according to the ordinance.
—Nehemiah 8:18b

My Dear Friend,

Hello, Sunday! Every day is Sunday here.

I was staring out my back window overlooking Lake Cheer while preparing to write to you when I noticed that Pal was down on the beach having a drink from the lake. He doesn't need to drink, but I catch him doing it from time to time—usually to appear casual while "investigating" the ducks that frequent the area. But then I saw Clarabelle's head pop out above the water in the middle of the lake. Well, Pal saw her and immediately thrust up his wings and flew over to where she appeared. For a moment, they touched noses as the two were obviously curious about each other. On the old earth, I used to think nothing was sweeter than seeing a puppy chasing a butterfly. But a winged horse tapping noses with a lake creature takes sweetness to a new level.

You have probably caught on that festivities are continuous on New Earth. Over at Linger, they are busy preparing for the "festival of multiples." Twins, triplets, and other multiples from all over are honored at this festival. It's funny how on the old earth we often couldn't tell some identical twins apart. Here we know and are known as individuals, so it's not a problem.

Not long ago I went to a big gathering in the Great City to honor the disciples. They were humbled by the attention. Each one of them is fascinating and—wait for it—witty. Oh, and the food at the party was magnificent. I particularly enjoyed the cheese-stuffed dates.

We have music festivals, art festivals, science festivals, dance festivals, storytelling festivals, theater festivals, animal parades, poetry festivals, literary festivals, and even comedians. Many of these events are filled with great food and drinks, and one can learn so much by attending. Some festivals are centered around old customs or centered around geographic areas and traditions, but some are focused on creating new traditions.

While many gatherings involve multitudes, we also enjoy small gatherings in our homes and even one-on-one meetings. And based on my last letter, you probably surmised that men don't just meet with men and women with women. My closest friend is male. Unlike me, he was married on old earth and his former wife (and kids) are here too. Because there is no basis for jealousy or favoritism in the Kingdom, it's normal and common for people of the opposite sex to spend time together. My male friends are as much fun to be with as my female friends. There's also no jealousy among friends, so my friends can be your friends too. I hope you are beginning to grasp the fact that there are no agendas, deceit, shadows, or withholding on New Earth. All gather in His name and in His light.

By the way, you took me to a wonderful festival in your district when we got together. It was a show and celebration of cut flowers. I enjoyed learning from the instructor who taught flower arrangement. Inviting me was so thoughtful of you.

Well, I must be off to Cheer for a meeting. I promise to write more next time.

Your friend forever,

Anne

P.S. Before I forget, I want to touch on a slightly related but deeper subject that may have crossed your mind. I know I've told you we often honor people. But I want to make sure you know that there is no competition for status or even for the King's attention. There is no striving to be better or smarter than someone else, no trying to prove yourself to be right or worthy, no trying to reverse a negative perspective you think others have of you. And while we esteem others more highly than ourselves, we never seek the favor of others over the favor of the King who is always attentive to us. Comparing and competing were part of our old sinful nature (born of pride, envy, greed, and covetousness). Now we live in the presence of the very God who is ultimately worthy of all honor and glory.

For this reason also, God highly exalted Him, and bestowed on Him the name which is above every name.
—Philippians 2:9

My Dear Friend,

When your future self visited me at Willow Bay, I learned these letters you received on the old earth were a blessing and comfort to you. I imagine that's probably why the King allowed me to send them. Even though I am thinking about you when I write these letters, He is thinking about you even more.

So this Sunday I want to talk about names. Let's start with that passage in scripture about the new name on a white stone. Because we saw things dimly on the old earth, I never knew what to make of that verse at the end of our Bibles.

Now I know He really did give each one of us a stone with a new name on it, inscribed by Christ Himself. The stone was something we got before we came here to dwell. It initially functioned as a ticket or Kingdom citizenship passport to enter New Earth. Now as you may recall from scripture, the name is a secret between each person and the King. So why would He give us a name that nobody else uses and no one around us knows? Turns out this matter is something quite indescribable. Though He loves us all, it is supremely individual and intimate that He did this for each of us. (One time I was alone with the King and He called me by my new name. It was truly thrilling!)

No one has the same new name, and our new name is an insight into what God was thinking about us at the time (before all time) He imagined us. The truth is He gave us each a name that conveys exactly who we were to be. Unfortunately, sin came into the world at the Fall, and none of us lived up to our full potential and purpose. Now we each make every effort to live up to the name and purpose He intended all along. In the lingo of old earth, talk about self-actualization!

Of course, no one has as many names as the King Himself. I typically refer to Him as King just because He oversees and sustains the Kingdom, and it was my favorite name for Him on the old earth. And while on old earth we loved hearing His names in scripture, here they have deeper meaning.

For example, it's quite awesome to know that He was not only there on old earth for us, but He was also here on New Earth before we were. That name (Jehovah-shammah) is even an alternate name for the Great City here on New Earth. That awareness was a comfort to us then, but now it's before our very eyes as a reminder that He transcends all our previous notions of time and space.

And Wonderful Counselor? Well, He still counsels us—and now we behold His wisdom and never doubt.

I won't go through all His names, but suffice it to say, they all have deeper and wider meaning than you now understand. And by the way, those names given in scripture were not exhaustive.

Perhaps you are starting to catch glimpses of the glory to come. Ask the Spirit to bring these glimpses to your mind as you go about your days, weeks, months, and years.

Your friend forever,

The Lord was going before them in a pillar of cloud by day to lead them on the way, and in a pillar of fire by night to give them light, that they might travel by day and by night.
—Exodus 13:21

My Dear Friend,

In previous letters, I've spoken a great deal about traveling around the Kingdom. Everyone gets around New Earth with ease. Some travel on foot because there's so much to see along the way. We don't get tired, leg cramps, or sore feet. I mostly travel this way, especially if going to the Great City. That's a long distance, but I always meet up with others who are heading there too. By walking, I get to know more people and have great times.

Having said that, I think I mentioned that on my trip to the Garden of Eden, I decided to go with Pal (my beautiful, winged horse). Traveling by horse makes a trip faster as we can go in a straight line. It's also quite scenic to see the landscape below from such heights. The vistas are spectacular. I'm not the only one with a winged horse. Many people who enjoyed the company of horses on old earth have their most beloved horses with them here. Some are earthbound, but some can fly.

I could travel on Sweetums as she is a dragon with wings. I don't do it often because she prefers to be by my side when we travel together. I take her almost everywhere I go. She's a constant companion.

I don't think I mentioned that there are trains here too. There are loads of people who love trains and even more who love to travel that way. People also use bikes, chariots, wagons, and other methods of travel. What we don't have are cars and buses. The roads are wide, clean, and sparkly. I've noticed that people tend to prefer a method that they used in their era on the old earth. Subsequently, you'll see anything from riding a donkey to rollerblades!

When summoned to the King, you're likely to be escorted by an angel or two. Those trips are quite rapid, but I'm not at liberty to say more than that.

Well, just a few more letters to go, so I'll try to spend a little more time on the architecture and music of the Kingdom. I know how much you love both.

Your friend forever,

Anne

And I saw the holy city, new Jerusalem, coming down
out of heaven from God, made ready as a bride adorned
for her husband.
—Revelation 21:2

My Dear Friend,

In previous letters, I've tried to describe some of the buildings on New Earth and even attempted to put words to the beauty of the Great City. Words really do fail to project just how gorgeous the whole place is. There's no graffiti or trash. No "bad parts of town." No neglect or abandonment. No eyesores. No overcrowding. Nobody here would want or permit such a thing. I guess that's because we do all things to His glory.

Let's see, I've told you about the art museum in New Italy, the library in New France, a telescope in New Spain, and my own home and district. I've told you about the Great City. Perhaps I have probably alluded to the fact that many of the architectural styles around New Earth are reflective of their old earth heritage and cultures. As you might expect, there are seaside villas in Italy and thatched cottages in New England. New North America has log homes, colonial-style homes, and contemporary homes. In New Central America, you can find sprawling adobe homes built around lovely courtyards. New Switzerland has lovely villages full of chalets. In New Australia, well, you find all kinds of styles there. On this earth you'll find golden domes, turrets, spires, mosaics, and gingerbread—it just depends on where you are.

One thing we don't have are churches or temples. That's because everywhere on New Earth is suitable for worshipping God and His King. After all, we are the Church, and He dwells with us.

But as wonderful as all the places on New Earth are, New Jerusalem is by far the pinnacle of beauty. But then, you'd expect that to be the case as it's fit for the King.

Your friend forever,

Sing praises to the Lord, who dwells in Zion;
Declare among the peoples His deeds.
—Psalm 9:11

My Dear Friend,

One of the things you loved on the old earth (and still love on New Earth) is music. I remember those wonderful times when you would sing in our church choir and even as a soloist from time to time. What a beautiful voice! I hope you are singing this Sunday.

As mentioned, New Earth is filled with music. All three towns in my district have at least one pub, and I love listening to pub performers. Often their shows end with everybody singing! And, of course, we have concerts, festivals, and events that center around music.

Famous singers of old earth (from all centuries, all cultures, and all genres) live on New Earth. For instance, that rascal of a nonbeliever who came to the Lord late in life, country music singer George Jones. I loved listening to him on the old earth, so I attended a concert he had recently in New North America. His love of the King (and his gratitude toward His saving grace) was proclaimed in his words and his music. The highlight of the concert was when the King Himself walked out onto the stage and George knelt before Him. The joy of that tender moment when the King placed his nail-pierced hand on the head of Jones was shared by everyone in attendance.

People sing bluegrass, opera, and Gregorian chant. There are quartets, quintets, soloists, and choirs (large and small). I can walk among the moors of New Scotland and I am bound to come across a bagpipe soloist walking along the road. The pipes echo all around. I can go to the Great City and hear the angel choirs or hear the Psalms performed. Or I can go to New South America and hear the pan flute. New Japan has amazing drumming. New Wales offers many a men's choir. Even friends visiting my home might break out in song or play an instrument. (We have all the instruments that existed through all the millennia on the old earth and some new things too!) And because most musicians travel frequently, you often don't even have to go to them. I've been to tons of music events in the amphitheater over in Grace. I especially appreciate the great pianists we have here. Handel himself performed at the latest concert I attended. The audience stood and sang the "Hallelujah" chorus that he played as the encore. It was so thrilling that angels appeared overhead to join us. And finally, the King Himself wrote a note to us across the sky (something He does from time to time). It said: I love you with an everlasting love. The guy standing next to me turned out to be one of the many men Handel ransomed from debtors' prison on the old earth. That guy told me that Handel departed old earth on Resurrection Sunday. I learn something new all the time here.

And are there other music composers? Oh my, we have those in spades. Some were composers on old earth, and some never wrote a single note on old earth but are now musically gifted. It's rather amusing to hear someone with a beautiful voice tell you that on the old earth they couldn't carry a tune in a bucket.

Just as on old earth, musicians tend to congregate and make music together. The only truly solo musicians I am aware of are in New Switzerland. Their yodeling and horn-playing are amazing.

And you know I loved the "old" hymns (which we still enjoy here), but the hymns from New Earth are so much richer and deeper. As I've said before, you're going to love it here.

Your friend forever,

For the faith of those chosen of God and the knowledge of the truth which is according to godliness, in the hope of eternal life, which God, who cannot lie, promised long ages ago.
—Titus 1:1b–2

My Dear Friend,

I am sitting in front of my large fireplace that contains a perpetual, smokeless fire. Fire in this realm does not need feeding once it's established and goes out only when you tell it to. (Yes, we can command the elements here.) Fire is multicolored. It does give off some heat, which is why Sweetums likes to lay in front of the hearth. She takes up most of the room, so I have my comfy chair next to the fireplace to let her stretch out and so Bosco has some room too.

Alas, this is my last opportunity to write to you. I feel that so much has been left unsaid. That's okay, isn't it? After all, you're going to want to experience the wonder of it all yourself anyway.

I think I want to leave you with this one thought: Even the very best day on the old earth would count as a sick day on New Earth (if we had sick days here). What He has in store for you is better than you can ever imagine. My mom used to say that to me when I was a little girl. I thought she was talking about my adult life on the old earth. While that life was certainly interesting (and filled with things both good and bad that I had never imagined), I now know that she was talking about the day when where He is, we will be also. (Of course, she's here and still tells me that.)

So, my friend, be sure to tell others to look to the Blessed Hope. Keep your eyes fixed on Jesus, and don't look back. Press on to the prize that awaits you in Him!

Forever and ever, amen,

P.S. Tickled pink! The Messenger that came for this letter ex-
changed it for a box. It contains a gorgeous white gown, shoes,
tiara, and gloves to wear at my much-anticipated personal parade
in the Great City. In the box was a handwritten note from the King,
who informed me that my animals are welcome as part of my en-
tourage. Hope to see you there!

About the author

After retiring from a decades-long successful business career, A.E. Ball surprised everyone, including herself, by venturing into fiction writing with the release of five novels under different pen names. Ms. Ball holds a B.S. from The Ohio State University, and an M.S. from Seattle Pacific University. A thoroughly western gal, she indulges her writing on a ten-acre farm in Western Washington where she maintains an educational exhibition garden with over two hundred roses.

Also from the author:
Beso Dulce by Rayanne Sinclair
Flight Risk by Rayanne Sinclair
Page Turner by Rayanne Sinclair
Steal Away by Rayanne Sinclair
The Companion by Pad Brotherton

www.ingramcontent.com/pod-product-compliance
Lightning Source LLC
Chambersburg PA
CBHW051313170626
46809CB00004B/1875